An Old-Fashioned ABC Book

ELIZABETH ALLEN ASHTON

An Old-Fashioned ABC Book

ILLUSTRATIONS BY
JESSIE WILLCOX SMITH

Puffin Books

PUFFIN BOOKS
Published by the Penguin Group
Viking Penguin, a division of Penguin Books USA Inc.,
375 Hudson Street, New York, New York 10014, U.S.A.
Penguin Books Ltd, 27 Wrights Lane, London W8 5TZ, England
Penguin Books Australia Ltd, Ringwood, Victoria, Australia
Penguin Books Canada Ltd, 10 Alcorn Avenue, Toronto, Ontario, Canada M4V 3B2
Penguin Books (N.Z.) Ltd, 182–190 Wairau Road, Auckland 10, New Zealand

Penguin Books Ltd, Registered Offices: Harmondsworth, Middlesex, England

First published in the United States of America
by Viking Penguin, a division
of Penguin Books USA Inc., 1990
Published in Puffin Books, 1992
3 5 7 9 10 8 6 4
Text copyright © Elizabeth Allen Ashton, 1990
All rights reserved

LIBRARY OF CONGRESS CATALOGING-IN-PUBLICATION DATA
Ashton, Elizabeth Allen.
An old-fashioned ABC book / by Elizabeth Allen Ashton ;
illustrated by Jessie Willcox Smith.   p. cm.
Originally published: New York, N.Y. : Viking Kestrel, 1990.
Summary: An alphabet book celebrating the art of Jessie Willcox
Smith, whose popular illustrations were featured on the covers of
"Good Housekeeping" throughout the 1920s and 1930s.
ISBN 0-14-054189-6 (pbk.)
[1. Alphabet.] I. Smith, Jessie Willcox, 1863–1935, ill.
II. Title.
[PZ7.A82801 1992]   [E]—dc20   91-29164

Printed in the United States of America
Set in Goudy Old Style

 is for Apple, all shiny and red.

Ann picked a whole basket with big brother Ted.

B is for Bonnet, tied with a bow, and
the basket of flowers for someone Beth knows.

is for Cat, Claire's mischievous friend. When she tries to help Claire, schoolwork comes to an end.

 is for Dishes, Dot's chore for the day.

Outside, Dan calls, "Are you done? Come and play!"

is for Envelope, with Ed's invitation,

saying, "Polly, please visit at Christmas vacation."

F is for Five of my favorite friends.

When we're together, the fun never ends.

 is for Goldfish, so orange and bright.

Kitty jumps at the bowl, so Greg holds on tight.

25 CENTS
35 CENTS IN CANADA

H is for Hammock, where Holly and I
watch dragons and castles in clouds drifting by.

I is for Ice skates. When Iris and I try our jumps and our spins, we can practically fly.

 is for Jump. Jenny misses the wave.

The sea is gentle today, so she can be brave.

K is for Kiss, but don't bump your noses!

Katy thanks Ken for the pretty pink roses.

 is for Luggage packed up for a trip.

Laura is all set for her journey by ship.

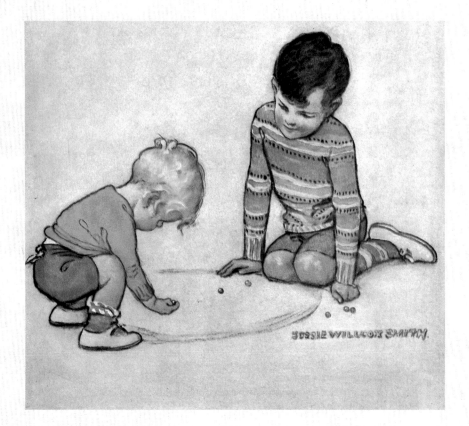

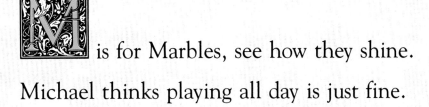 is for Marbles, see how they shine.

Michael thinks playing all day is just fine.

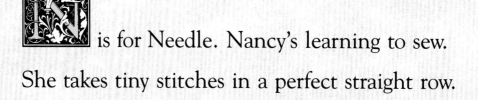 is for Needle. Nancy's learning to sew.

She takes tiny stitches in a perfect straight row.

O is for Oatmeal, Olive's hot breakfast treat.

Here's a spoonful with honey for Teddy to eat.

is for Pail. Peter plays by the sea.

He promised to build a big castle for me.

JESSIE WILLCOX SMITH

Q is for Queenie, our faithful friend,

who reads right beside us from beginning to end.

 is for Reading in our big chair. I read

to Ruth from a book that we share.

S is for Seashore, where Sue plays with sand.
She likes how it feels when it sifts through her hand.

 is for Tulips, all in a row.

Terry cares for them tenderly so they will grow.

U is for Umbrella to keep off the rain. I stay nice and dry, though I'm blown down the lane.

is for Valentine I leave at the door

to tell you I love you, each day more and more.

W is for Wind, whipping up such a noise.

Wanda covers her ears and holds tight to her toys.

X in my letter is the sign for a kiss
that says I love you to the friend that I miss.

 is for Yard I rake every day, making

piles of leaves where my friends jump and play.

is for Zephyr, a warm breeze blowing by, stirring soft scents of flowers, chasing clouds 'cross the sky.